The Little Prince

Antoine De Saint-Exupery

Srishti
PUBLISHERS & DISTRIBUTORS

Srishti Publishers & Distributors
N-16, C. R. Park
New Delhi 110 019
srishtipublishers@gmail.com

First published 1999
Reprinted 2012

Printed and bound in India

TO LEON WORTH

I ask the forebearance of the children who may
read this book for dedicating it to a grown-up.
My first and most serious reason is that he
is the best friend I have in the world.
My second reason is that this grown-up
understands everything, even books about children.
And my third reason is that he lives in France
where he is hungry and cold.
He needs cheering up.
If all these reasons are not enough,
I will dedicate the book to the little boy
from whom this grown-up grew.
All grown-ups were children once –
although few of them remember it.
And so I correct my dedication:

TO LEON WORTH
WHEN HE WAS A LITTLE BOY

A. DE S.-E., 1944

THE LITTLE PRINCE

CHAPTER ONE

Once when I was six years old I saw a beautiful picture in a book about the primeval forest called *True Stories*. It showed a boa constrictor swallowing an animal. Here is a copy of the drawing.

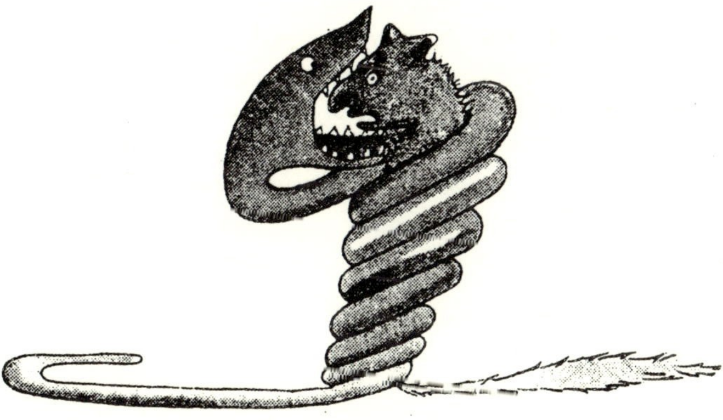

The book stated: 'Boa constrictors swallow their prey whole without chewing it whereupon they can no longer move and sleep for six months digesting it.'

I then reflected deeply upon the adventures in the jungle and in turn succeeded in making my first drawing with a colour pencil. My drawing No. 1 was like this:

I showed my masterpiece to the grown-ups and asked them if my drawing frightened them.

They answered: 'Why should anyone be frightened by a hat?' My drawing did not represent a hat. It was supposed to be a boa constrictor digesting an elephant. So I made another drawing of the inside of the boa constrictor to enable the grown-ups to understand. They always need explanations. My drawing No. 2 looked like this:

The grown-ups then advised me to give up my drawings of boa constrictors, whether from the inside or the outside, and to devote myself instead to geography, history, arithmetic and grammar. Thus it was that I gave up a magnificent career as a painter at the age of six. I had been disappointed by the lack of success of my drawing No. 1 and my drawing No. 2. Grown-ups never understand anything by themselves and it is rather tedious for children to have to explain things to them time and again.

So I had to choose another job and I learnt to pilot aeroplanes. I flew more or less all over the world. And indeed geography has been extremely useful to me. I am able to distinguish between China and Arizona at a glance. It is extremely helpful if one gets lost in the night.

As a result of which I have been in touch, throughout my life, with all kinds of serious people. I have spent a lot of time with grown-ups. I have seen them at very close quarters which I'm afraid has not greatly enhanced my opinion of them.

Whenever I met one who seemed reasonably clear-sighted to me, I showed them my drawing No 1, which I had kept, as an experiment. I wanted to find out whether he or she was truly understanding. But the answer was always: 'It is a hat.' So I gave up mentioning boa constrictors or primeval forests or stars. I would bring myself down to his or her level and talk about bridge, golf, politics and neckties. And the grown-up would be very pleased to have met such a sensible person.

CHAPTER TWO

Thus I lived alone, with no one I could really talk to, until I had an accident in the Sahara Desert six years ago. Something broke down in my engine. And since there was neither a mechanic nor a passenger with me, I prepared myself for a difficult but what I hoped would be a successful repair. It was a matter of life or death for me. I had scarcely enough drinking water for a week.

On the first night, I fell asleep on the sand, a thousand miles from any human habitation. I was far more isolated than a shipwrecked sailor on a raft in the middle of the ocean. So you can imagine my surprise at sunrise when an odd little voice woke me up.

It said: 'Please . . . draw me a sheep.'

'What?'

'Draw me a sheep.'

I jumped up, completely thunderstruck. I rubbed my eyes, blinked hard and looked carefully around me. And I discovered an extraordinary little boy watching me gravely. Here is the best portrait I was able to draw of him later. But of course, my drawing is not half as charming as its model. It is not my fault. I had been discouraged by grown-ups in my career as a painter when I was six years old, and I hadn't learnt to draw anything with the exception of boas from the outside and boas from the inside.

I therefore stared in total astonishment at this

sudden apparition. Do not forget that I was a thousand miles away from any inhabited region.

But my little chap did not seem to be either lost or dead tired or dying of hunger, thirst or fear. He did not look like a child lost in the middle of the desert, a thousand miles from any inhabited region.

When I finally managed to speak, I said to him: 'But . . . what are you doing here?'

Whereupon he repeated softly and gravely: 'Please draw me a sheep '

When a mystery is too overpowering, one dare not disobey. Absurd as it seemed to me a thousand miles from any human habitation and in danger of death, I took a sheet of paper and my fountain pen out of my pocket. But I suddenly remembered that my studies had been concentrated on geography, history, arithmetic and grammar, so I told the little chap (a little crossly) that I did not know how to draw.

He replied: 'That doesn't matter. Draw me a sheep.'

Since I had never drawn a sheep I drew for him one of the two pictures I had drawn before. That of the boa constrictor from the outside. And I was astounded to hear the little fellow saying: 'No! No! I don't want an elephant inside a boa. A boa constrictor is a very dangerous creature and an elephant is very cumbersome. Everything is very small where I live. I need a sheep. Draw me a sheep.'

So I drew.

He looked at it carefully and said: 'No. That one is already very sick. Draw me another one.'

And I drew.

My little friend said gently and indulgently: 'Don't you see that is not a sheep, it is a ram. It has horns . . . '

Once again, I made another drawing.

But it was rejected too, like the previous ones.

'This one is too old. I want a sheep that will live for a long time.'

My patience had run out by then as I was in a hurry to start dismantling my engine as soon as possible, so I scribbled this drawing. And I explained: 'That is only the box. The sheep you asked for is inside.'

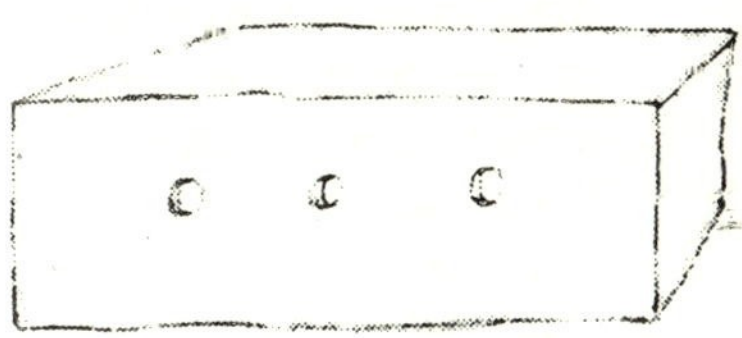

But I was very surprised to see the face of my young judge lighting up: 'That is exactly the way I wanted it. Do you think this sheep will need a lot of grass?'

'Why?'

'Because where I live everything is so small . . . '

'There should be enough grass for him. I have given you a very small sheep.'

He bent his head over the drawing: 'Not so small that . . . Look. He has gone to sleep.'

And that is how I met the little prince.

CHAPTER THREE

It took me a long time to find out where he came from. The little prince who asked me so many questions never seemed to hear mine. It is thanks to the odd word, here and there, that everything was revealed to me.

For instance, when he saw my aeroplane for the first time (I shall not draw my aeroplane; that would be far too complicated for me), he asked me: 'What is that object?'

'It is not an object. It flies. It is an aeroplane. It is my aeroplane.'

And I was proud to be able to tell him that I could fly.

He cried out then: 'What! You dropped down from the sky?'

'Yes,' I replied modestly.

'Oh! That is funny.' And the little prince broke into a lovely peal of laughter which annoyed me no end. I like my misfortunes to be taken seriously. 'So you too come from the sky. From which planet?'

I immediately perceived a ray of light in the mystery of his presence and at once questioned him:

'So you've come from another planet?'

But he didn't reply. He nodded gently whilst gazing at my aeroplane.

'It is true that on that you can't have come from very far away . . . '

And he sank into a long reverie. Then, taking my sheep out of his pocket, he contemplated his treasure.

You can imagine how my curiosity was aroused by this half confidence about 'the other planets'. So I tried to find out a little more.

'Where do you come from, my little fellow? Where is this "where I live" of which you speak? Where do you want to take my sheep?'

After a thoughtful silence, he replied: 'What I like about the box you have given me is that he can use it as his house at night.'

'Of course. And if you are good, I shall also give you a rope to tie him up during the day. And a post to tie him to.'

But the little prince seemed shocked by my proposal.

'Tie him up? What a funny idea.'

'But if you do not tie him up, he will wander off and get lost.'

My friend burst out laughing again: 'But where would he go?'

'Anywhere. Just straight ahead.'

Whereupon the little prince remarked gravely: 'It wouldn't matter. Everything is so small where I live.' And, perhaps a little wistfully, he added: 'Straight ahead of oneself, one cannot go very far . . . '

CHAPTER FOUR

Thus I had learned a second very important thing. That his planet of origin was scarcely larger than a house.

But that did not really surprise me very much. I knew full well that apart from the large planets, such as Earth, Jupiter, Mars and Venus, which have been given names, there are hundreds of others which are sometimes so small that it is difficult to see them through a telescope. When an astronomer discovers one of them, he does not give it a name but a number. He might call it, for example, 'Asteroid 325'.

I have serious reasons to believe that the little prince's planet of origin was the asteroid known as B-612. This asteroid has only been observed once through a telescope by a Turkish astronomer in 1909.

At the time, he organised a great demonstration of his discovery at an International Astronomical Congress. But because of his Turkish attire, nobody believed him. Grown-ups are like that.

Fortunately for the reputation of Asteroid B-612, however, a Turkish dictator imposed European costume upon his subjects under pain of death. So the astronomer repeated his demonstration in 1920, dressed in an elegant suit. And this time everybody was convinced.

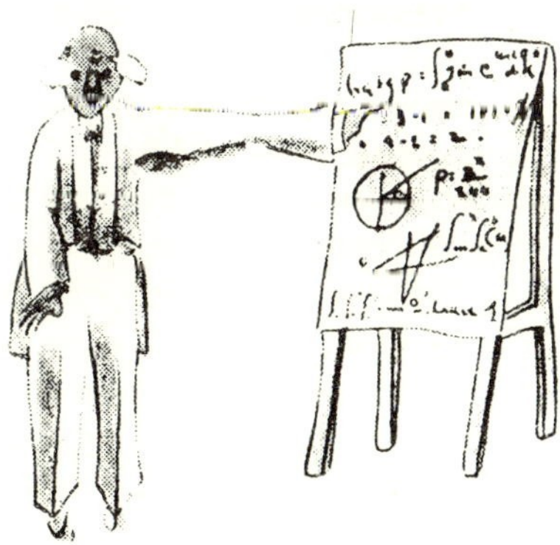

If I have told you these details about Asteroid B-612 and revealed its number to you, it is on account of grown-ups. Grown-ups love figures. When you talk to them about a new friend, they never ask questions about essential matters. They never say to you: 'What does his voice sound like? What games does he prefer? Does he collect butterflies?' They ask you: 'How old is he? How many brothers does he have? How much does he weigh? How much money does his father earn?' It is only then that they feel they know him. If you were to mention to grown-ups: 'I've seen a beautiful house built with pink bricks, with geraniums on the windowsills and doves on the roof . . . ' they would not be able to imagine such a house. You would have to say to them: 'I saw a house worth a hundred thousand pounds.' Then they would exclaim: 'Oh! How lovely.'

Thus if you said to them: 'The proof that the little prince really existed was that he was enchanting, that he laughed and that he wanted a sheep. Now when you want a sheep, it proves that you exist,' they will shrug their shoulders and will treat you as if you were a child. But if you say to them: 'The planet he came from was Asteroid B-612,' then they will be convinced and leave you alone with their questions. That is the way they are. One must not hold it against them. Children should show great understanding towards grown-ups.

But, of course, for those of us who understand life, we could not care less about figures. I should have liked to start this story like a fairy tale. I should have liked to say: 'Once upon a time there was a little prince who lived on a planet scarcely bigger than himself and who had need of a friend.' For those who understand what life is all about, it would have seemed closer to the truth.

For I do not want my book to be read carelessly. I have experienced so much grief in setting down these memories. Six years have already elapsed since my little friend left me, with his sheep. If I am attempting to describe him, it is in order not to forget him. It is sad to forget a friend. Not every one has had a friend. And I could become like grown-ups who are only concerned with figures. That is why I have bought a box of paints and some pencils. It is hard to take up drawing again at my age, having never made any attempts other than drawing a boa from the outside and a boa from the inside at the age of six. I shall certainly endeavour to make my portraits as true to life as possible. But I am not at all sure of succeeding. One drawing is all right, another shows no resemblance at all to its subject. The height is not right either. Here, the little prince is too tall. There, he is too small. And I am not sure about the colour of his suit. So I persist by trial and error and to the best of my ability. I shall also make mistakes about some more important details. But I must be forgiven for that. My friend never explained anything to me. Perhaps he thought I was like him. But, unfortunately, I cannot see sheep through boxes. Perhaps I am a little like grown-ups. I am getting old.

CHAPTER FIVE

Each day, I learnt something about the planet, about the little prince's departure from it, about his journey. The information would come very slowly, following the course of the little prince's thoughts. Thus it was that on the third day, I heard about the catastrophe of the baobabs.

Once again, it was thanks to the sheep, for suddenly the little prince questioned me as if seized by a grave doubt: 'It is true, is it not, that sheep eat little shrubs?'

'Yes, that is true.'

'Ah! I'm glad.'

I did not understand why the fact that sheep eat shrubs was so important. But the little prince added: 'Therefore, they also eat baobabs?'

I pointed out to the little prince that baobabs are not little bushes but trees as tall as churches, and that even if he were to take a whole herd of elephants with him, the herd would not be able to eat up one single baobab.

The little prince laughed at the idea of a herd of elephants: 'One would have to pile them up on top of one another.' But then he remarked wisely: 'Before they grow to such a size,

baobabs start out by being small.'

'That is true. But why do you want your sheep to eat the small baobabs?'

He answered me: 'Oh! come, come!' as if this was self-evident.

I had to exert considerable mental effort to work the problem out for myself.

It seemed that on the little prince's planet, as on all

planets, there were good plants and bad plants. Good seeds come from good plants and bad seeds come from bad plants. But seeds are invisible. They re[illegible] dormant in the depth of the earth until one of them suddenly decides to wake up. It stretches itself, timidly at first, and then begins to push a charming little sprig inoffensively towards the sun. If it is merely a sprout of radish or a sprig of rosebush, it can be left to grow as it wishes. But if it is a weed, it should be torn out at once, as soon as it is recognised. It so happens that there were some terrible seeds on the little prince's planet . . . they were baobab seeds. The soil of the planet was infested with them. But if you intervene too late, you will never get rid of a baobab. It spreads over the entire planet. Its roots bore clear through it. And if the planet is too small and if there are too many baobabs, the planet explodes.

'It is a question of discipline,' said the little prince to me later on. 'When you have finished your toilet in the morning, it is time to attend to the planet's toilet with great care. One must pull out the baobabs very regularly as soon as they can be distinguished from the rosebushes they resemble so closely when they are very young. It is very tedious work but also very easy.'

And one day he advised me to try and make a beautiful drawing so as to impress all this upon the children where I live. He said to me: 'If they travel one day, it might be of use to them. It may be convenient sometimes to put off one's work until another day. But in the case of baobabs, it is always catastrophic to do so. I knew of a planet inhabited by

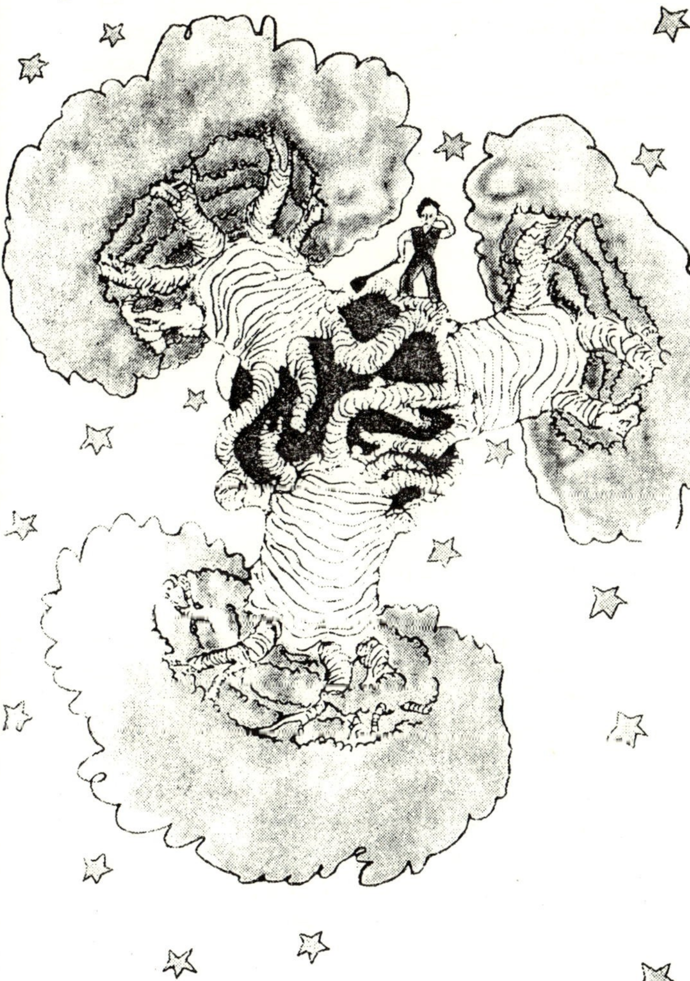

So, basing my work upon the descriptions of the little prince, I made the drawing you have just seen. I don't like to sound like a moralist. But the danger of baobabs is so little known and the risks are so considerable to whomever might get lost on an asteroid that, for once, I make an exception to my reserve. I say: 'Children. Beware of baobabs!' It is in order to warn my friends of a danger of which they, like me, have been unaware for so long, that I have worked so hard over this drawing. My lesson was worth it. You may ask yourselves: Why are there no other drawings in this book as impressive as the drawing of baobabs? The answer is quite simple: I have tried but with the others have not had the slightest success. When I drew the baobabs, I was driven by a feeling of urgency.

CHAPTER SIX

Ah! little prince. Bit by bit I came to understand your sad little life . . . For a long time, your only entertainment had been the pleasure of watching sunsets. I learnt that new detail on the morning of the fourth day, when you said to me: 'I am very fond of sunsets. Let us go and watch a sunset . . . '

'But we must wait . . . '

'Wait for what?'

'Wait for the sun to set.'

You looked very surprised at first, and then you laughed to yourself and said to me: 'I keep on thinking I am at home.'

Yes indeed. When it is midday in the United States, the sun, as everyone knows, is setting in France. One would just have to travel in one minute to France to be able to watch the sun setting there. Unfortunately, France is too far away for that. But on your tiny little planet, all you needed to do was to move your chair a few steps. And you could watch the twilight falling whenever you felt like it . . .

'One day, I watched the sun setting forty-four times,' you told me. And a little later, you added: 'You know . . . when one is so terribly sad, one loves sunsets . . .'

'The day you watched those forty-four sunsets, were you that sad?' I asked.

But the little prince made no reply.

CHAPTER SEVEN

On the fifth day, and once again thanks to the sheep, this secret of the little prince's life was revealed to me. Without any preamble and as if it were the result of a silently thought out problem, he asked me abruptly: 'A sheep, if it eats bushes, does it eat flowers too?'

'A sheep eats anything it comes across.'

'Even flowers with thorns?'

'Yes, even flowers with thorns.'

'Then the thorns – what use are they?'

I did not know. I was very busy trying to unscrew a bolt which had got stuck in my engine. I was deeply worried as the breakdown of my plane was beginning to look extremely serious to me, my drinking water was running out fast and I could only fear the worst.

'The thorns – what use are they?'

The little prince never let go of a question once he had raised it. I was annoyed about my bolt and I answered with the first thing that came to my mind: 'Thorns are quite useless. Flowers have them out of sheer spite.'

'Oh!'

But after a moment of silence, he said with a kind of resentfulness: 'I don't believe you. Flowers are weak. They are naïve. They reassure themselves as best they can. They believe that their thorns are terrible . . .'

I did not answer. At that instant I was saying to

myself: 'If this bolt continues to resist me, I shall knock it off with a hammer.'

Once again, the little prince intruded upon my thoughts: 'And do you actually believe that flowers . . . '

'No! No! I don't believe anything. I just answered any old how. I am busy with serious matters.'

He stared at me in total astonishment.

'Serious matters?'

He could see me with a hammer in my hand and my fingers black with engine grease, bending down over an object which seemed to him extremely ugly.

'You talk just like grown-ups.'

This made me feel a little ashamed of myself.

Relentlessly he added: 'You are confusing everything . . . mixing everything up.'

He was really quite angry. He shook his golden locks in the wind: 'I know of a planet where there is a red-faced gentleman. He has never smelled a flower. He has never looked at a star. He has never loved anybody. He has spent all his time adding up figures. And, all day, he keeps on repeating, like you: "I am busy with serious matters. I am busy with serious matters," over and over again. And he swells up with pride. But he is not a man, he is a mushroom.'

'A what?'

'A mushroom.'

The little prince was now pale with anger.

'For millions of years flowers have been growing thorns. And for millions of years sheep have still been eating flowers. And is it not worth trying to understand why they go to such lengths to grow thorns which are

of no use to them? Is the war between sheep and flowers not important? Not more serious and more important than the sums of the red-faced gentleman? And if I know of a flower which is unique in the world and grows nowhere other than on my planet and that a small sheep can destroy it with a single bite, just like that, one morning, without realising what it is doing, is that not important?'

He blushed and continued: 'If someone loves a flower of which there is only one on the millions and millions of stars, it is enough to make him happy when he looks at them for he can say to himself:

'My flower is somewhere out there . . . " But if the sheep eats the flower, it is for him as if, all of a sudden, all the stars went dark! And you think that is not important!'

He could say no more because he was overcome with tears. Night had fallen. I had dropped my tools. I couldn't have cared less about my hammer, my bolt, thirst or death. There was on a star, a planet, mine, the Earth, a little prince to be comforted! I took him in my arms and rocked him gently. I said to him, 'The flower you love is in no danger . . . I shall draw you a muzzle for your sheep . . . I shall draw you a fence for your flower . . . I . . . ' I did not really know what to say to him. I felt very awkward. I did not know how to reach him, how to catch up with him . . . The land of tears is so mysterious.

CHAPTER EIGHT

I soon learnt to know this flower better. There had always been very simple flowers on the little prince's planet, with a single ring of petals, occupying very little space and no trouble to anybody. They would appear one morning in the grass and fade away in the evening. But one day, from a seed blown from no one knew where, a new flower had come up; and the little prince had watched very closely over the small shoot which was not at all like any of the other shoots on his planet. It could have been a new kind of baobab. But the plant soon stopped growing and started to develop a flower. The little prince, watching the growth of an enormous bud, sensed that this could well lead to a miraculous apparition, but the flower continued her preparations for her beauty in the shelter of her green chamber. She chose her colours with great care. She dressed slowly, carefully arranging her petals one by one. She didn't wish to appear all crumpled, like a poppy. She only wished to appear in the full glory of her beauty. Oh yes! She was very vain! Her mysterious preparations had lasted for days and days. And then one morning when the sun was rising, she suddenly showed herself.

And having worked so hard and taken such care, she yawned and said: 'Ah! I'm only half awake . . . Forgive me . . . I'm still quite dishevelled . . . '

But the little prince couldn't restrain his admiration and exclaimed: 'Oh, how beautiful you are!'

'Am I not?' the flower replied gently. 'And I was born at the same time as the sun . . . '

The little prince had to admit that she was not excessively modest but she was so enchanting!

'I believe it's time for breakfast,' she added a moment later, 'would you be kind enough to attend to my needs . . . '

And the little prince, totally abashed, at once fetched a can of fresh water and sprinkled the flower.

Thus it was that she began from the outset to torment him with her demanding vanity.

One day, for example, referring to her four thorns, she said to the little prince: 'Let them come, those tigers with their claws!'

'But there are no tigers on my planet,' objected the little prince, 'and anyway, tigers don't eat weeds.'

'But I am not a weed,' the flower replied sweetly.

'Please forgive me . . . '

'I am not afraid of tigers but I hate draughts. You wouldn't have a screen for me, by any chance?'

'A horror of draughts . . . that's really bad luck for a plant,' remarked the little prince, thinking to himself, 'This flower is indeed a very complex creature . . . '

'In the evening I want you to put me under a glass dome. It is very cold here where you live. And rather uncomfortable. Now where I come from . . . '

Too late she interrupted herself. She had arrived as a seed. She could not have known anything about other worlds. Embarrassed at having been discovered preparing such a naïve lie, she coughed a couple of times so as to confuse the little prince.

'Where is the screen?'

'I was going to fetch it but you were talking to me!'

Whereupon she coughed a little more so that he should feel remorse.

So the little prince, in spite of the goodwill his love engendered towards her, came gradually to doubt her. He had taken words of no importance seriously and became very unhappy.

'I shouldn't have listened to her,' he confided to me one day, 'one should never listen to flowers. One must admire them and breathe their fragrance. Mine perfumed all my planet, but I did not know how to enjoy her. That tale of claws which irritated me so much should simply have touched my heart . . . '

And he confided further

'At the time, I was unable to understand anything! I should have based my judgement upon deeds and not words. She cast her fragrance and her radiance over me. I should never have run away from her! I should have guessed at the affection behind her poor little tricks. Flowers are so inconsistent! But I was too young to know how to love her.'

CHAPTER NINE

I suspect that for his escape, he took advantage of the migration of wild birds. On the morning of his departure; he put his planet in perfect order. He carefully swept his active volcanoes. He possessed two active volcanoes and they were very convenient for heating his breakfast in the morning. He also had a volcano which was extinct. But as he pointed out: 'You never know!' So he also cleaned out the extinct volcano. If they are properly swept, volcanoes burn gently and regularly, without any eruptions. Volcanic eruptions are like chimney fires. On Earth, of course, we are far too small to sweep our volcanoes. That is why they cause us so much trouble.

The little prince tore up, not without a sense of sorrow, the last little baobab shoots. He believed that he would never have to return. But all these familiar activities seemed very precious to him on that last morning. And, when he watered the flower for the last time and prepared to place her under her glass dome, he felt like crying.

'Goodbye,' he said to the flower.

But she did not answer him.

'Goodbye,' he said again.

The flower coughed. But it was not because she had a cold.

'I've been silly,' she whispered at last. 'Please forgive me. Try to be happy.'

He was surprised by the absence of reproaches. He just stood there, quite bewildered, with the dome poised in mid-air. He did not understand this quiet sweetness.

'Of course, I love you,' the flower said to him. 'If you were not aware of it, it was my fault. That is not important. But you have been just as foolish. Try to be happy . . . Leave that dome alone. I don't want it any longer.'

'But the wind . . . '

'My cold is not that bad . . . The cool night air will do me good. I am a flower.'

'But what about animals . . . '

'I shall have to put up with a few caterpillars if I want to see butterflies. I understand they are very beautiful. Otherwise, who will ever call upon me? You will be far away. As to large animals, I am not afraid of them. I have my claws.' And, as naïve as ever, she showed her four thorns. Then she added: 'Don't hang about so, it's irritating. You have decided to leave, so leave.'

For she didn't want him to see her crying. She was a very proud flower . . .

CHAPTER TEN

He found himself in the neighbourhood of the asteroids, 325, 326, 327, 328, 329 and 330. So he started by visiting them to look for an occupation and to add to his knowledge.

The first one was inhabited by a king. Clad in purple and ermine, he was seated on a throne, both simple and majestic.

'Ah! Here comes a subject,' exclaimed the king when he spied the little prince.

And the little prince wondered to himself: 'How can he recognise me since he has never seen me before?'

He did not know that for kings the world is greatly simplified. To them, all men are subjects.

'Come a little closer so that I may see you better,' said the king, inordinately proud of having someone to be king over at last.

The little prince looked around to find a place to sit down; but the entire planet was covered by the magnificent ermine robe. So he remained standing and, since he was tired, he yawned.

'It is contrary to etiquette to yawn in the presence of a king,' said the monarch. 'I forbid it.'

'I cannot help it,' replied the little prince in confusion. 'I have come on a long journey and I haven't slept at all . . . '

'In which case,' said the king, 'I order you to yawn. I have not seen anybody yawning for years. Yawns are a curiosity to me. Come now! Yawn again. It is an order.'

'You are frightening me . . . I cannot yawn any more . . .' said the little prince, blushing.

'Hum! Hum!, replied the king. 'Then I order you sometimes to yawn and sometimes to . . . '

He spluttered a bit and seemed vexed.

For the king attached considerable importance to his authority being respected. He tolerated no disobedience. He was an absolute monarch. But as he was very kind, he gave reasonable orders.

'If I ordered a general,' he would say, 'if I ordered a general to change himself into a sea-bird, and if the general did not obey, it wouldn't be the general's fault. It would be my fault for ordering him to do the impossible.'

'May I sit down?' asked the little prince shyly.

'I order you to sit down,' replied the king, majestically gathering a fold of his ermine robe around him.

But the little prince was puzzled. The planet was tiny. Over what could this king really rule?

'Sire . . . ' he began, ' . . . please excuse my asking you a question . . . '

'I order you to put your question to me,' the king was quick to reply.

'Sire . . . over what do you rule?'

'Over everything,' replied the king very simply.

'Over everything?'

The king made a sweeping gesture taking in his own planet, the other planets and the stars.

'Over all that?' said the little prince.

'Over all that,' replied the king.

For he was not only an absolute monarch but a universal one.

'And the stars obey?'

'Of course,' said the king. 'They obey immediately. I do not tolerate insubordination.'

The little prince marvelled at such power. Had he possessed it, he could have watched not forty-four, but seventy-two or even one hundred or two hundred sunsets in one and the same day, without ever having to move his chair! And as he was feeling rather sad, remembering his small abandoned planet, he plucked up the courage to ask the king a favour.

'I should like to see a sunset . . . Please, do me that kindness . . . Order the sun to set . . . '

'If I were to order a general to fly from one flower to another like a butterfly, or to write a tragedy, or to change himself into a sea-bird, and if the general did not carry out the order, which one of us would be at fault?'

'It would be you,' said the little prince firmly.

'Exactly. One must demand of each and every one what he or she is capable of. Authority is first and foremost based on reason. If you order your people to throw themselves into the sea, you will have a revolution on your hands. I have the right to demand obedience because my orders are reasonable ones.'

'What about my sunset?' the little prince reminded him, for he never forgot a question once he had asked it.

'You shall have your sunset. I shall demand it. But, in accordance with scientific government, I shall wait until conditions are favourable.'

'And when will that be?' asked the little prince.

'Hum! Hum!' replied the king, consulting his big calendar. 'Hum! Hum! it will be around . . . around . . . it will be this evening about twenty minutes to eight. And you shall see how well I am obeyed.'

The little prince yawned. He regretted having to miss the sunset but he was becoming a little bored.

'I have nothing more to do here,' he said to the

king, 'so I'll be on my way!'

'Don't leave,' said the king, who was to proud of having a subject. 'I'll make you a minister!'

'A minister of what?'

'Of . . . of justice!'

'But there is nobody here to judge!'

'We do not know that,' said the king. 'I haven't yet made a complete tour of my kingdom. I am very old, and walking makes me very tired, but there is no room here for a carriage.'

'Oh! but I have already looked,' said the little prince, bending down to give one more glance to the other side of the planet, just to be sure

'Then you shall judge yourself,' answered the king. 'That is the most difficult thing of all. It is far more difficult to judge oneself than to judge others. If you succeed in judging yourself rightly, then indeed you are very wise.'

'As far as I am concerned,' said the little prince, 'I can judge myself anywhere. I do not have to live here.'

'Hum! Hum!' said the king. 'I believe that somewhere on my planet, there is an old rat. I can hear him at night. You can judge that old rat. You will condemn him to death from time to time. Thus his life will depend upon your justice. But on each occasion you will spare him so as to keep him alive. He is the only one we have.'

'I,' replied the little prince, 'do not like to condemn anything to death and I think I'll be on my way.'

'No,' said the king.

The little prince, having completed his preparations, had no wish to hurt the feelings of the old monarch.

'If Your Majesty wishes to be promptly obeyed, you should give me a reasonable order. You could, for example, order me to be gone in less than a minute. It seems to me that conditions are favourable . . . '

As the king said nothing, the little prince hesitated a moment and then, with a sigh, took his leave.

'I make you my ambassador,' the king called after him in haste.

He had a magnificent air of authority.

'Grown-ups are very strange,' said the little prince to himself, continuing on his journey.

CHAPTER ELEVEN

The second planet was inhabited by a conceited individual.

'Aha! Here comes an admirer!' he exclaimed as, from afar, he caught sight of the little prince. For conceited men see all other men as admirers.

'Good-morning,' said the little prince. 'You are wearing a funny kind of hat.'

'It is a hat for salutes,' the conceited man replied, 'to raise when people acclaim me. Unfortunately, nobody ever comes this way.'

'Indeed?' said the little prince who did not understand what the conceited man was talking about.

'Clap your hands,' the conceited man advised.

The little prince clapped his hands. The conceited man raised his hat in a modest salute.

'This is more fun that my visit to the king,' the little prince said to himself. And he tried clapping his hands again. The conceited man once again raised his hat in salute.

After five minutes of this exercise the little prince grew tired of the monotony of the game.

'And to make you lower your hat , what should one do?' he asked.

But the conceited man didn't hear him. Conceited men only hear praise.

'Do you really admire me very much?' he asked the little prince.

'What does "admire" mean?'

'To admire means that you consider me the handsomest, the best dressed, the richest and the most intelligent man on this planet.'

'But you are all alone on your planet!'

'Do me this kindness. Admire me all the same!'

'I admire you,' said the little prince with a slight shrug of his shoulders, 'but why should that mean so much to you?'

And the little prince went away.

'Grown-ups are really very odd,' he said to himself, as he continued on his journey.

CHAPTER TWELVE

The next planet was inhabited by a drunkard. This visit was a very short one, but it affected the little prince with deep sadness.

'What are you doing here?' he said to the drunkard whom he found sitting silently in front of a collection of bottles, some empty and some full.

'I am drinking,' answered the drunkard lugubriously.

'Why are you drinking?' the little prince asked.

'In order to forget,' replied the drunkard.

'To forget what?' enquired the little prince, who was already feeling sorry for him.

'To forget that I am ashamed,' the drunkard confessed, hanging his head.

'Ashamed of what?' asked the little prince who wanted to help him.

'Ashamed of drinking!' concluded the drunkard, withdrawing into total silence.

And the little prince went away, puzzled.

'Grown-ups really are very, very odd,' he said to himself as he continued his journey.

CHAPTER THIRTEEN

The fourth planet belonged to a businessman. He was so busy that he didn't even look up when the little prince arrived.

'Good-morning,' the little prince said to him. 'Your cigarette has gone out.'

'Three plus two make five. Five plus seven make twelve. Twelve plus three make fifteen. Good-morning. Fifteen plus seven make twenty-two. Twenty-two plus six make twenty-eight. No time to light it again. Twenty-six plus five make thirty-one. Phew! Then that makes five hundred and one million, six hundred and twenty-two thousand, seven hundred and thirty-one.'

'Five hundred million of what?'

'Eh? Are you still there? Five hundred and one million of . . . I don't remember . . . I have so much work! I am a serious man, I don't amuse myself with balderdash! Two and five make seven . . . '

'Five hundred and one million of what?' repeated the little prince, who never in his life let go of a question once he had asked it

The businessman raised his head.

'During the fifty-four years that I have been living on this planet, I have only been disturbed three times. The first time was twenty-two years ago by a cockchafer who dropped down from goodness knows where. He made the most awful noise and I made four errors in

my sums. The second time was eleven years ago by an attack of rheumatism. I don't get enough exercise. I have no time for slacking. I'm a serious man. The third time . . . well, this is it! As I was saying, five hundred and one million . . . '

'Million of what?'

The businessman suddenly realised that there was no hope of being left in peace.

'Of those small objects one sometimes sees in the sky.'

'Flies?'

'Oh no. Small glittering objects.'

'Bees?'

'Oh no. Small golden objects that set lazy men to idle dreaming. But I am a serious man! I have no time for idle dreaming.'

'Ah! You mean the stars?'

'Yes, that's it. The stars.'

'And what do you do with five hundred million stars?'

'Five hundred and one million, six hundred and twenty-two thousand, seven hundred and thirty-one. I am a serious man. I am accurate.'

'And what do you do with five hundred million stars?'

'Five hundred and one million, six hundred and twenty-two thousand, seven hundred and thirty-one.'

'And what do you do with them?'

'What do I do with them?'

'Yes.'

'Nothing. I own them.'

'You own the stars?'

'Yes.'

'But I have already seen a king who . . . '

'Kings *own* nothing. They *reign over*. It is quite different.'

'And what use is it to you to own the stars?'

'It makes me rich.'

'And what is the point of being rich?'

'It enables me to buy other stars, if anybody can find any.'

'This man,' the little prince said to himself, 'reasons a bit like my drunkard.' None the less, he put a few more questions.

'How can one own stars?'

'Whose are they?' the businessman asked peevishly.

'I don't know. They don't belong to anyone.'

'In which case they are mine, because I was the first person to think of it.'

'Is that sufficient?'

'Of course it is. When you find a diamond that belongs to nobody, it is yours. When you discover an island that belongs to no one, it is yours. When you are the first to have an idea, you take out a patent on it: it is yours. And I own the stars because nobody else before me thought of owning them.'

'That is logical,' said the little prince. 'And what do you do with them?'

'I manage them, I count them and recount them,' said the businessman. 'I am a man concerned with matters of consequence!'

The little prince was still not satisfied.

'If I owned a silk scarf, I could put it around my neck and take it away with me. If I owned a flower I could pick it and take it away with me. But you cannot pick stars!'

'No, but I can put them in the bank.'

'Whatever does that mean?'

'It means that I write down the number of my stars on a piece of paper. And then I put it in a drawer and lock it with a key.'

'And is that all?'

'It is enough!'

'Quite amusing,' thought the little prince. 'Rather poetic. But an exercise of no real importance.'

The little prince's ideas about what was important were very different from those of grown-ups.

'I myself own a flower which I water every day,' he told the businessman. 'I own three volcanoes which I clean out every week. I always include the one which is extinct. One never knows. It is good for my volcanoes and good for the flower I own. But you are of no use to the stars . . . '

The businessman opened his mouth but found nothing to say, and the little prince went on his way.

'Grown-ups are certainly absolutely extraordinary,' he said to himself as he continued on his journey.

CHAPTER FOURTEEN

The fifth planet was very strange. It was the smallest one of all. There was just enough room for a lamp-post and a lamplighter. The little prince wondered what could be the use of a lamp-post and a lamplighter somewhere in the sky, on a planet without houses or people.

None the less, he said to himself, 'Perhaps, the lamplighter is absurd. However, he is not as absurd as the king, the conceited man, the businessman and the drunkard. For at least his work has some meaning. When he lights his streetlamp, it is as if he brought one more star to life, or one more flower. When he extinguishes his lamp, it puts the flower or the star to sleep. It is a beautiful occupation. And since it is beautiful, it is truly useful.'

When he arrived on the planet, he saluted the lamplighter respectfully.

'Good-morning, sir. Why have you just put out your lamp?'

'Those are the orders,' replied the lamplighter. 'Good-morning.'

'What are the orders?'

'The orders are that I put out my lamp. Good-evening.'

And he lit his lamp again.

'But why have you just lit it again?'

'Those are the orders,' replied the lamplighter.

'I don't understand,' said the little prince.

'There is nothing to understand,' said the lamplighter. 'Orders are orders. Good-morning.'

And he put out his lamp.

Then he mopped his brow with a handkerchief decorated with red squares.

'My calling is a terrible one. In the old days it was reasonable. I put out the lamp in the morning and lit it again in the evening. For the rest of the day, I could relax and for the rest of the night I could sleep . . . '

'And the orders have been changed since that time?'

'The orders have not been changed,' said the lamplighter. 'And that is the tragedy! From year to year, the speed of the planet's rotation has increased considerably and the orders have not been changed!'

'And so?' asked the little prince.

'Well, now that the speed has reached one rotation per minute, I do not have a second's rest. I have to light up and put out my lamp once a minute.'

'That is very funny! Where you live, a day only lasts one minute!'

'It is not funny at all,' said the lamplighter. 'We have already been talking together for a whole month.'

'A month?'

'Yes. Thirty minutes. Thirty days! Good-evening.'

And he lit his lamp again.

As the little prince watched him, he felt he had come to love this lamplighter, so faithful to his orders. He remembered the sunsets which he himself used to seek by simply moving his chair. He wanted to help his friend.

'You know . . . I believe there is a way which would allow you to take a rest whenever you wanted to . . . '

'I always want to,' said the lamplighter.

For one can be both faithful and lazy.

The little prince continued: 'Your planet is so small that you can walk all around it in three strides. You just have to walk slowly enough to stay always in the sun. When you want to take a rest, you will walk . . . and the day will last for as long as you like.'

'That wouldn't help me very much,' said the lamplighter. 'The one thing I like in life is to sleep.'

'That is unfortunate,' said the little prince.

'That is indeed unfortunate,' said the lamplighter. 'Good-morning.'

And he put out his lamp.

'That man,' said the little prince to himself as he continued his journey, 'that man would be despised by all the others, by the king, be the conceited man, by the drunkard, by the businessman. But he is the only one who does not seem ridiculous to me. Perhaps it is because he is not only concerned with himself.'

With a sigh of regret, he said to himself once again: 'That man is the only one I could have made my friend. But his planet is really too small. There is not enough room for two . . . '

What the little prince would not admit to himself was that he was sorry to leave this planet, blessed as it was with one thousand and four hundred and forty sunsets every day.

CHAPTER FIFTEEN

The sixth planet was a planet ten times larger. It was inhabited by an old gentleman who wrote voluminous books.

'Oh look! Here comes an explorer!' he cried out when he saw the little prince.

The little prince sat down on the table, catching his breath. It seemed he had been travelling for so long!

'Where do you come from?' asked the old gentleman.

'What is this thick book?' said the little prince, disregarding the question. 'What are you doing here?'

'I am a geographer,' said the old gentleman.

'What is a geographer!'

'A geographer is a scholar who knows the location of all the seas, the rivers, the cities, the mountains and the deserts.'

'Now that is extremely interesting,' said the little prince. 'That is at long last a real profession!' And he cast a quick look around him at the geographer's planet. Never before had he seen such a magnificent planet.

'Your planet is very beautiful. Are there any oceans?'

'I have no way of knowing,' said the geographer.

'Oh!' The little prince was disappointed. 'And any mountains?'

'I really couldn't tell you that either,' said the geographer.

'And cities and rivers and deserts?'

'I have no way of knowing that either,' said the geographer.

'But you are a geographer!'

'Exactly,' said the geographer, 'but I am not an explorer. I have no explorers on my planet. It is not the geographer's task to count the cities, the rivers, the mountains, the oceans and the deserts. The geographer is far too important to waste his time browsing around. He never leaves his office. But he receives explorers. He questions them and notes down what they recall of their travels. And if the recollections of one of them seem interesting to him, the geographer orders an inquiry into the explorer's moral character.'

'But why?'

'Because an explorer who told lies would bring into disrepute the geographer's books. As would an explorer who drank too much.'

'But why? asked the little prince.

'Because drunkards see double. As a result, the geographer would note two mountains where, in fact, there was only one.'

'I know someone,' said the little prince, 'who would make a bad explorer.'

'That is possible. Even when the moral character of the explorer is shown to be satisfactory, an investigation is ordered into his discovery.'

'One goes to check it?'

'No. That would be too complicated. But the explorer is requested to furnish proof. If, for example, the discovery is that of a big mountain, he is required to bring back some large stones from it.' Suddenly, the geographer became very excited. 'But you, you've come a long way! You are an explorer! You must describe your planet to me!'

And the geographer, having opened his register, sharpened his pencil. One started off by noting the explorer's story in pencil. And when the explorer had provided the required proof, the information was filled in in ink.

'Well?' asked the geographer expectantly.

'Oh! where I live,' said the little prince, 'it is not very interesting because it is so small. I have three volcanoes. Two are active and the third is extinct. But one never knows.'

'One never knows,' said the geographer.

'I also have a flower.'

'We don't record flowers,' said the geographer.

'Why not! It is the prettiest thing on my planet!'

'Because flowers are ephemeral.'

'What does "ephemeral" mean?'

'Geographies,' said the geographer, 'are the most precious of all books. They are never out of fashion. A mountain rarely changes its place. It is very rare for an ocean to empty itself of its waters. We write of eternal things.'

'But extinct volcanoes can wake up,' the little prince interrupted. 'What does "ephemeral" mean?'

'Whether volcanoes are extinct or active amounts to the same thing for us,' said the geographer. 'What matters to us is the mountain. It does not change.'

'But what does "ephemeral" mean,' the little prince repeated once again, since he had never in his life given up a question once he had raised it.

'It means "in danger of early disappearance".'

'My flower is in danger of early disappearance?'

'Of course it is.'

'My flower is ephemeral,' the little prince said to himself, 'and she has only four thorns with which to defend herself against the world! And I have left her all alone on my planet!'

That was his first moment of regret. But he took courage once again.

'What place would you advise me to visit now?' he asked.

'The planet Earth,' replied the geographer. 'It has a good reputation . . . '

And the little prince went away, thinking of his flower.

CHAPTER SIXTEEN

So the seventh planet was the Earth.

The Earth is not just an ordinary planet! There are one hundred and eleven kings (not to mention the Negro kings, of course), seven thousand geographers, nine hundred thousand businessmen, seven and a half million drunkards, three hundred and eleven million conceited individuals – in other words, approximately two thousand million grown-ups.

To give you an idea of the size of the Earth, I shall explain that before the invention of electricity, throughout the six continents, a veritable army of 462,511 lamplighters had to be maintained for the streetlamps. Seen from a little distance, the effect was magnificent. The movements of this army were regulated like those of a ballet. First came the turn of the lamplighters of New Zealand and Australia. Then, having lit their lamps, they would go off to sleep. Next, the lamplighters of China and Siberia would join the dance. After which they too would disappear into the wings. Then came the turn of the lamplighters of Russia and India. Then those of Africa and Europe. Then those of South America. Then those of North America. And they never made a mistake in the order of their entry on to the stage. It was fabulous. Only the man in charge of the single lamp at the North Pole and his colleague responsible for the single lamp at the South Pole could enjoy a carefree life of laziness: they only worked twice a year.

CHAPTER SEVENTEEN

When one wants to be funny, one may have to lie a little bit from time to time. I haven't been quite honest in talking to you about the lamplighters. I am running the risk of giving a false idea about our planet to those who do not know it. Men occupy very little space on the Earth. If the two billion inhabitants occupying the planet were to stand upright and crowded together, as at a meeting, they could easily live on a public square twenty miles long and twenty miles wide. All humanity could be piled up on a tiny islet in the Pacific.

Grown-ups of course will never believe you. They think that they take up a lot of space. They consider themselves as important as baobabs. You should invite them to make their own calculations. They adore figures and would be pleased. But do not waste *your* time on such a chore. It is unnecessary. I know you trust me.

So when the little prince arrived on the Earth, he was very surprised not to see any people. He was beginning to fear he had come to the wrong planet when a coil, pale gold as the moon, moved in the sand.

'Good-evening,' said the little prince politely.

'Good-evening,' said the snake.

'What planet have I fallen on?' asked the little prince.

'On the planet Earth, in Africa,' replied the snake.

'Oh! . . . Then there are no people on Earth?'

'This is the desert. There are no people in the desert. The Earth is big,' said the snake.

The little prince sat down on a stone and looked up at the sky

'I wonder,' he said, 'if the stars are lit up so that each one of us can find his own star again. Look at my planet. It is right above us . . . But how far away it is!'

'It is beautiful,' said the snake; 'why have you come here?'

'I am having some difficulties with a flower,' the little prince replied.

'Oh!' said the snake.

And they remained silent.

'Where are the men?' said the little prince, at last resuming the conversation. 'One feels rather lonely in the desert.'

'It is just as lonely among men,' said the snake.

The little prince gazed at him for a long time.

'You're a strange animal,' he said at last. 'You are as thin as a finger . . . '

'But I am more powerful than a king's finger,' said the snake.

The little prince smiled. 'You do not look very powerful . . . you don't even have paws . . . you cannot even travel.'

'I can carry you farther than a ship,' said the snake.

He twined himself around the little prince's ankle, like a golden bracelet.

'Whomever I touch I send back to the earth from

which they came,' he added. 'But you are pure and innocent and come from a star.'

The little prince said nothing.

'I feel sorry for you, so weak on this Earth of granite. I may be able to help you one day, if you become too homesick for your own planet. I can . . . '

'Oh! I understand you perfectly,' said the little prince. 'But why do you talk in riddles all the time?'

'I solve them all,' said the snake.

And they both fell silent.

CHAPTER EIGHTEEN

The little prince crossed the desert and met with only one flower. A flower with very few petals, a flower of no importance . . .

'Good-morning,' said the little prince.

'Good-morning,' said the flower.

'Where are the men?' the little prince enquired politely.

The flower had once seen a caravan passing.

'Men? I believe there are about six or seven of them. I caught a glimpse of them several years ago. But one never knows where to find them. The wind blows them around. They have no roots which makes their life rather trying.'

'Goodbye,' said the little prince.

'Goodbye,' said the flower.

CHAPTER NINETEEN

The little prince climbed a high mountain. The only mountains he knew of were the three volcanoes, and they only reached up to his knees. And he used the extinct volcano as a foot-stool. 'From the top of a mountain as high as this one,' he said to himself, 'I should be able to see the whole planet at one glance, and all the people . . . ' But the only things he could see were peaks of rock as sharp as needles.

'Good-morning,' he said politely.

'Good-morning . . . Good-morning . . . Good-morning,' answered the echo.

'Who are you?' asked the little prince.

'Who are you . . . Who are you . . . Who are you . . .' answered the echo.

'Be my friends, I am all alone,' he said.

'I am all alone . . . all alone . . . all alone . . .' answered the echo.

'What a strange planet!' he thought to himself. 'It is quite dry, covered with peaks, salty and inhospitable. And the people have no imagination. They just repeat whatever one says to them . . . On my planet I had a flower: she was always the first to speak.'

CHAPTER TWENTY

However, the little prince, having walked for a long time through the desert, the rocks and the snow, at last came upon a road. And all roads lead to men.

'Good-morning,' he said, coming upon a garden full of roses.

'Good-morning,' said the roses.

The little prince gazed at them. They all resembled his flower.

'Who are you?' he asked in amazement.

'We are roses,' said the roses.

'Oh!' exclaimed the little prince.

And he was suddenly overcome with sadness. His flower had told him that she was the only one of her kind in the universe. And here were five thousand of them, all alike, in one single garden!

'She would be rather resentful,' he thought to himself, 'if she could see this . . . she would cough and cough and pretend she was dying so as to avoid being thought ridiculous. And I would have to pretend to nurse her, for otherwise she would really let herself die . . . in order to humiliate me.'

And he said to himself once again: 'I thought I was rich, with a flower unique in the world, whereas in fact all I had was a common rose. That, and my three volcanoes which came up to my knees, of which one is

perhaps extinct forever . . . that doesn't make me a very great prince.'

And, lying in the grass, he cried.

CHAPTER TWENTY-ONE

It was then that the fox appeared.

'Good-morning,' said the fox.

'Good-morning,' the little prince replied politely, though when he turned around, he saw nothing.

'I am here,' said the voice, 'under the apple tree . . .'

'Who are you?' said the little prince. 'You are very pretty . . . '

'I am a fox,' said the fox.

'Come and play with me,' suggested the little prince. 'I am so terribly sad . . . '

'I cannot play with you,' said the fox. 'I am not tame.'

'Oh! I'm so sorry,' said the little prince. But, after some thought, he asked: 'What does "tame" mean?'

'You do not live here,' said the fox. 'What are you looking for?'

'I am looking for men,' said the little prince. 'What does "tame" mean?'

'Men,' said the fox, 'have rifles and they hunt. It is a real nuisance. They also raise chickens. Those are the only activities they are interested in. Are you looking for chickens?'

'No,' said the little prince. 'I am looking for friends. What does "tame" mean?'

'It is something which is too often forgotten,' said the fox. 'It means to establish ties . . . '

' "To establish ties"? '

'That's right,' said the fox. 'To me, you are still just a little boy like a hundred thousand other little boys. And I have no need of you. And you have no need of me, either. To you, I am just a fox like a hundred thousand other foxes. But if you tame me, we shall need one another. To me, you will be unique. And I shall be unique to you.'

'I'm beginning to understand,' said the little prince. 'There is a flower . . . I think she has tamed me . . . '

'Possibly,' said the fox. 'One sees all sorts of things on Earth . . . '

'Oh! But this is not on Earth,' said the little prince.

The fox seemed puzzled.

'On another planet?'

'Yes.'

'Are there any hunters on that planet?'

'No.'

'That's interesting! And any chickens?'

'No.'

'Nowhere is perfect,' sighed the fox. Presently, he returned to his theme. 'My life is monotonous. I hunt chickens and men hunt me. All chickens are alike and all men are alike. So I get a little bored. But if you tame me, my life will be full of sunshine. I shall recognise the sound of a step different from all others. The other steps send my hurrying underground. Yours will call me out of my burrow like the sound of music. And look yonder! Do you see the cornfields? I do not eat bread. Wheat is of no use to me. Those cornfields don't remind me of anything. And I find that rather sad! But you have hair the colour of gold. So it will be marvellous when you have tamed me! Wheat, which is also golden, will remind me of you. And I shall love the sound of the wind in the wheat . . . '

The fox became silent and gazed for a long time at the little prince.

'I beg of you . . . tame me!' he said.

'Willingly,' the little prince replied, 'but I haven't got much time. I have friends to discover and a lot of things to understand.'

'One can only understand the things one tames,' said the fox. 'Men have no more time to understand anything. They buy ready-made things in the shops. But since there are no shops where you can buy friends, men no longer have any friends. If you want a friend, tame me!'

'What should I do?' asked the little prince.

'You must be very patient,' replied the fox. 'First you will sit down at a little distance from me, like that, in the grass. I shall watch you out of the corner of my eye and you will say nothing. Words are a source of misunderstandings. But every day, you can sit a little closer to me . . . '

The next day, the little prince returned.

'You should have come back at the same time,' said the fox. 'If for example you come at four o'clock in the afternoon, I shall start feeling happy at three o'clock. As the time passes, I shall feel happier and happier. At four o'clock, I shall become agitated and start worrying; I shall discover the price of happiness.

But if you come at just any time, I shall never know when I should prepare my heart to greet you . . . One must observe certain rites.'

'What is a rite?' asked the little prince.

'It is something which is all too often forgotten,' said the fox. 'It is what makes one day different from other days, one hour different from other hours. For example, there is a rite among my hunters. On Thursdays they go dancing with the village girls. So Thursday is a marvellous day for me. I can take a walk as far as the vineyards. But if the hunters were to go dancing just any day, every day would be like any other day for me and I would never have a holiday.'

Thus it was that the little prince tamed the fox. And when the time came for his departure, the fox said: 'Oh! . . . I shall cry.'

'It is your own fault,' said the little prince. 'I wished you no harm but you wanted me to tame you.'

'Yes, indeed,' said the fox.

'But you are going to cry!' said the little prince.

'That is so,' said the fox.

'Then it has not helped you in any way!'

'It has helped me,' said the fox, 'because of the colour of the wheatfields.' Then he added: 'Go and have another look at the roses. And you will understand that yours is indeed unique in all the world. Then you will come back to say goodbye to me and I shall tell you a secret as a gift.'

The little prince went off to look at the roses again.

'None of you is at all like my rose. As yet you are nothing,' he said to them. 'Nobody has tamed you

and you have tamed no one. You are like my fox when I first encountered him. He was just a fox like a hundred thousand other foxes. But I made him my friend and now he is unique in the world.'

And the roses were greatly embarrassed.

'You are beautiful but you are empty,' he continued. 'One cannot die for you. To be sure, an ordinary passer-by would believe that my very own rose looked just like you, but she is far more important than all of you because she is the one I have watered. And it is she that I have placed under a glass dome. And it is she that I have sheltered behind a screen. And it is for her that I have killed the caterpillars (except for the two or three saved to become butterflies). And it is she I have listened to complaining or boasting or sometimes remaining silent. Because she is my rose.'

And he went back to the fox.

'Goodbye,' he said

'Goodbye,' said the fox. 'Now here is my secret. It is very simple. It is only with one's heart that one can see clearly. What is essential is invisible to the eye.'

'What is essential is invisible to the eye,' the little prince repeated, so as to be sure to remember.

'It is the time you lavished on your rose which makes your rose so important.'

'It is the time that I lavished on my rose . . . ' said the little prince, so as to be sure to remember.

'Men have forgotten this basic truth,' said the fox. 'But you must not forget it. For what you have tamed, you become responsible forever. You are responsible for your rose . . . '

'I am responsible for my rose . . . ' the little prince repeated, so as to be sure to remember.

CHAPTER TWENTY-TWO

'Good-morning,' said the little prince.

'Good-morning,' said the railway signalman.

'What do you do here?' asked the little prince.

'I sort out the travellers, in bundles of a thousand,' said the signalman. 'I shunt the trains carrying them, now to the right, now to the left.'

And a brilliantly lit-up express train, roaring like thunder, shook the signal-box as it rushed by.

'They are in great hurry,' said the little prince. 'What are they looking for?'

'The locomotive driver doesn't even know himself,' said the signalman.

And a second brilliantly lit express train thundered by in the opposite direction.

'Are they already coming back? asked the little prince.

'Those are not the same ones,' said the signalman. 'It is an exchange.'

'They were not satisfied where they were?'

'No one is ever satisfied where he is,' said the signalman.

And they heard the roaring thunder of a third brilliantly lit express train

'Are they pursuing the first travellers?' asked the little prince.

'They are pursing nothing at all,' said the signalman. 'They sleep in there, or they yawn. Only the children press their noses against the window-panes.'

'Only children know what they are looking for,' said the little prince. 'They dote on a rag doll and it becomes very important to them, and if it is taken away from them, they cry . . . '

'They are lucky,' said the signalman.

CHAPTER TWENTY-THREE

'Good-morning,' said the little prince.

'Good-morning,' said the merchant.

He was a merchant selling sophisticated pills intended to quench one's thirst. If a single pill was swallowed once a week, the need to drink disappeared.

'Why are you selling those?' asked the little prince.

'Because it saves a lot of time,' said the merchant. 'Experts have worked it all out. You save fifty-three minutes a week.'

'And what does one do with those fifty-three minutes?'

'Whatever one wishes.'

'If I had fifty-three minutes to spend,' said the little prince, 'I would walk very slowly towards a spring of fresh water . . . '

CHAPTER TWENTY-FOUR

It was now eight days since I had broken down in the desert and I listened to the story of the merchant while drinking the last drop of my water supply.

'Ah!' I said to the little prince, 'these memories of yours are quite delightful, but I haven't yet succeeded in repairing my plane. I have no water left to drink and I too would be happy if I could walk slowly towards a spring of fresh water!'

'My friend the fox said to me . . . '

'My dear little chap, this has nothing to do with a fox!'

'Why?'

'Because we are going to die of thirst . . . '

He didn't follow my reasoning and replied: 'It is good to have had a friend, even if one is going to die. I am very happy to have had a fox as a friend . . . '

'He does not realise the danger,' I said to myself. 'He is never hungry or thirsty. All he needs is a little sunshine . . . '

But he looked at me and responded to my thoughts.

'I too am thirsty . . . Let's go and look for a well . . . '

I made a gesture of weariness; it is absurd to look for a well, at random, in the immensity of the desert. None the less we started walking.

We walked for hours in silence; darkness fell and the stars began to come out. Due to my thirst I was slightly feverish and saw them as in a dream. The little prince's last words came dancing back into my mind.

'So you are thirsty, too?' I asked him.

But he did not reply to my question and said simply: 'Water may also be good for the heart . . . '

I didn't understand his answer but remained silent. I knew only too well that there was no point in questioning him.

He was tired and sat down. I sat down beside him. After a short silence he spoke again: 'The stars are beautiful because of a flower one cannot see . . . '

I replied 'of course' and I looked at the sand dunes under the moonlight in silence.

'The desert is beautiful,' he added . . .

And it was true. I have always loved the desert. One sits down on a sand dune, sees nothing, hears nothing. Yet one can feel a silent radiation . . .

'What makes the desert so beautiful,' said the little prince, 'is that it hides a well, somewhere . . . '

I was surprised by a sudden awareness the sand's mysterious radiation. When I was a little boy, I lived in a very old house and a legend told us that a treasure was buried there. To be sure, nobody had ever discovered it nor even searched for it, perhaps. But it cast an enchantment over that house. My home was hiding a secret in the depths of its heart . . .

'Yes,' I said to the little prince, 'be it a house, the stars or the desert, the source of their beauty cannot be seen!'

'I am glad that you agree with me,' he said.

As the little prince fell asleep, I took him in my

arms and started walking again. I was deeply moved. It seemed to me I was carrying a very fragile treasure. It even seemed to me that there was nothing more fragile on all the Earth. In the moonlight I gazed at the pale forehead, the closed eyes, the locks of hair trembling in the breeze, and said to myself: 'What I see here is nothing but a shell. What is most important is invisible . . .'

As his lips opened slightly with the suspicion of a half-smile, I said to myself once again: 'What moves me so deeply about this little prince sleeping here is his loyalty to a flower, the image of a rose shining through his whole being like the flame of a lamp, even when he is asleep . . .' And I felt him to be more fragile still. Lamps should be protected with great care: a gust of wind can extinguish them . . .

And I walked on and at daybreak I discovered the well.

CHAPTER TWENTY-FIVE

'Men,' said the little prince, 'crowd into express trains without knowing what they are looking for. So they become agitated and rush round in circles . . . ' After a pause, he added: 'It is not worth the trouble . . . '

The well we had reached did not look like the usual wells of the Sahara. The Sahara wells are simple holes dug in the sand. This one looked like a village well. But there was no village here and I thought I was dreaming.

'How strange,' I said to the little prince, 'everything is ready: the pulley, the bucket and the rope . . . '

He laughed, touched the rope and set the pulley working. And the pulley moaned like an old weather-cock when the wind has been asleep for a long time.

'Can you hear?' said the little prince. 'We have awakened the well and it is singing . . . '

I did not wish him to make an effort: 'Leave it to me,' I said to him, 'it is too heavy for you.'

Slowly I pulled up the bucket and planted it firmly on the edge of the well. I could still hear the singing of the pulley in my ears and in the water, which was still trembling, I could see the shimmering of the sun.

'I am thirsty for this water,' said the little prince, 'give me some of it to drink . . . '

And I understood what he had been looking for!

I raised the bucket to his lips. He drank with his eyes closed. It was as sweet as a festival treat. This water was something entirely different from ordinary nourishment. It was born from the walk under the stars, the singing of the pulley and the effort of my arms. It was good for the heart, like a gift. When I was a little boy, the lights of the Christmas tree, the music of the Midnight Mass, the sweetness of the smiling faces, all made up the radiance of the Christmas gift I received.

'The men where you live,' said the little prince, 'grow five thousand roses in the same garden . . . and they do not find what they are looking for . . .'

'They do not find it,' I replied.

'And yet, what they are looking for could be found in a single rose or in a little water.'

'Yes, indeed,' I replied.

And the little prince added: 'But the eyes are blind. One must look with the heart.'

I had drunk the water. I was breathing easily. The sand at sunrise is the colour of honey. And I was very much enjoying this honey colour. Why then was I feeling such grief . . .

'You must keep your promise,' said the little prince softly as he sat down beside me again.

'What promise?'

'You know . . . a muzzle for my sheep . . . I am responsible for this flower . . .'

So I took my rough sketches out of my pocket. The little prince looked at them and laughed as he said: 'Your baobabs are a bit like cabbages.'

'Oh!' And I had been so proud of my baobabs!

'Your fox . . . its ears . . . they look a bit like

horns . . . and they are too long!'

And he laughed again.

'You are unfair, little prince. Remember I could only draw boa constrictors from the outside and boa constrictors from the inside.'

'Oh! That's enough,' he said. 'Children understand.'

So I drew a muzzle with a pencil. And my heart ached when I gave it to him. 'You have plans I know nothing about . . . '

But he didn't answer. Instead, he said to me: 'You know, my descent to the Earth . . . tomorrow will be its anniversary . . . ' Then, after a short silence he added: 'I came down very near here . . . '

And he blushed.

And once again, without understanding why, I had a strange feeling of sorrow. However, a question came to my mind.

'So it is not by mere chance that on the morning I met you, eight days ago, you were wondering around all by yourself one thousand miles from any human habitation? You were returning to the place where you had landed?'

The little prince blushed again.

And I added a little hesitantly: 'Perhaps because of the anniversary? . . . '

The little prince blushed again. He never answered questions, but when one blushes, it means 'yes' does it not?

'Oh dear! I am a bit frightened . . . ' I said to him.

Reassuringly, he replied: 'Now you must work. You must get back to your engine. I shall wait for you here. Come back tomorrow evening . . . '

But I was not reassured. I remembered the fox. One runs the risk of crying a bit if one allows oneself to be tamed . . .

CHAPTER TWENTY-SIX

Beside the well, there was the ruin of an old stone wall. When I came back from my work on the following evening, I saw from some distance my little prince sitting on top of it, his legs dangling. And I heard him saying: 'Don't you remember? It was not quite here!'

No doubt another voice answered him since he replied: 'Yes! Yes! it is the right day, but not the right spot . . . '

I continued walking towards the wall but still could neither see nor hear anybody. Yet the little prince answered once again: ' . . . Yes, of course. You will see where my track begins in the sand. Just wait for me there. I shall be there tonight.'

I was a mere twenty metres from the wall and yet I could see nothing. After a short silence the little prince spoke again: 'Is your poison good? Are you sure it will not make me suffer for too long?'

I stopped in my tracks, my heart aching, but I still did not understand.

'Now, go away . . . ' he said. 'I want to get down!'

Whereupon I dropped my eyes to the foot of the wall and and what I saw made me leap into the air! It was there, raising its head towards the little prince, one of those yellow snakes which can kill you in a matter of seconds. Groping in my pocket for my revolver, I started running, but because of the noise I

was making the snake gently slipped back into the sand, like the dying spray of a fountain, and, in no apparent hurry, disappeared among the stones with a light metallic sound.

I reached the wall just in time to catch my little prince in my arms; his face was white as snow.

'What does this mean?' I asked him. 'Why are you talking with snakes?' I had untied the golden muffler which never left him. I had moistened his temples and given him a little water to drink. And now I didn't dare ask him any more questions. He looked at me gravely and put his arms around my neck. I could feel his heart beating like the heart of a dying bird, shot with someone's rifle.

He said to me: 'I'm so glad you discovered what was the matter with your engine. Now you can go home . . . '

'How did you know?'

In fact, I was coming to tell him that, contrary to all expectations, my endeavours had been successful!

He didn't reply to my question but whispered: 'I too am going home today . . . '

Then he added a little sadly: 'It is much farther away . . . It is far more difficult . . . '

I could sense that something quite extraordinary was about to happen. I was holding him tightly in my arms like a child and yet it seemed to me that he was slipping straight down into an abyss, and I could do nothing to prevent it . . .

His gaze was grave and lost in the distance.

'I have your sheep. And I have the box for the

sheep. And I also have the muzzle . . . '

And he smiled sadly.

I waited for a long time. I could feel that little by little, he was getting warmer.

'My dear little man, you were afraid . . . '

Of course he had been frightened! But he laughed gently.

'I shall be far more frightened this evening . . . '

Once again I was frozen by a sense of something irreparable. And I realised that I couldn't bear the thought of never hearing that laughter again. It was like a spring of fresh water in the desert for me.

'Little prince, I want to hear you laughing again . . .'

But he said to me: 'Tonight, it will be a year . . . My star will be just above the spot where I came down a year ago . . . '

'Little prince,' I said, 'tell me it is just a bad dream, this story of a snake and of a meeting and a star . . . '

But he did not answer my question. Instead he said to me: 'What is important cannot be seen . . . '

'Yes, I know . . . '

'Just as for the flower. If you love a flower which happens to be on a star, it is sweet at night to gaze at the sky. All the stars are a riot of flowers.'

'Yes, I know . . . '

'It is the same with the water. The draught you gave me was just like music, because of the pulley and the rope . . . you remember don't you . . . it was sweet.'

'Yes, I know . . . '

'At night, you will gaze at the stars. Where I live everything is so small that I cannot show you where mine is. It is better like that. My star will just be one of the stars for you. So you will love looking up at them all. They will all be your friends. And I have a present for you . . . '

He laughed again.

'Ah! Little prince, my dear little prince, I love to hear that laughter!'

'Precisely, that will be my gift . . . as it was with the water . . . '

'What are you saying?'

'The stars mean different things to different people. For some they are nothing more than twinkling lights in the sky. For travellers they are guides. For scholars they are food for thought. For my businessman they are wealth. But for everyone the stars are silent. Except from now on just for you . . . '

'What do you mean?'

'When you look up at the sky at night, since I shall be living on one of them and laughing on one of them, for you it will be as if all the stars were laughing. You and only you will have stars that can laugh!'

And as he said it he laughed.

'And when you are comforted (time soothes all sorrows) you will be happy to have known me. You will always be my friend. You will want to laugh with me. And from time to time you will open your window, just for the pleasure of it . . . And your friends will be astonished to see you laughing whilst gazing at the sky. And so you will say to them, "Yes, stars always make me laugh." And they will think you are crazy. I shall have played a very naughty trick on you . . .'

And once again he laughed.

'It will be as if I had given you, instead of stars, a lot of little bells that can laugh . . .'

And again he laughed. Then he became serious again. 'Tonight . . . you know . . . do not come.'

'I shall not leave you.'

'I shall seem to be in pain. I shall look as if I were dying. It is like that. Do not come to see that. There's just no point . . . '

'I shall not leave you.'

But he was worried.

'I am telling you this . . . partly because of the snake. It must not bite you . . . Snakes are vicious creatures. They can bite just for the fun of it . . . '

'I shall not leave you.'

But a thought reassured him.

'It is true that they have no poison left for a second bite . . . '

That night I did not see him set out. He had left without a sound. When I managed to catch up with him, he was walking along with a quick and resolute step.

He merely said to me: 'Oh! You are here . . .

And he took me by the hand. But he was still worrying.

'You should not have come. You will be unhappy. I shall look as if I were dead and it will not be true . . . '

I said nothing.

'You must understand. It is too far. I cannot carry this body with me. It is too heavy.'

I said nothing.

'It will look like an old abandoned shell . . . Not anything to be sad about . . . '

I said nothing.

He was a little discouraged. But he made one last effort.

'It will be nice, you know. I too shall look at the stars. All the stars will be wells with rusty pulleys. All the stars will pour me some water to drink . . . '

I said nothing.

'It will be such fun! You will have five hundred million little bells, I shall have five hundred million springs of fresh water . . . '

And he too said nothing more because he was crying . . .

'Here it is. Let me go on by myself.'

And he sat down because he was afraid.

Then he said: 'You know . . . my flower . . . I am responsible for her. And she is so weak, so trusting. She has four tiny thorns to protect herself against the world . . . '

I sat down because I could not remain standing any longer.

He said: 'There now . . . That is all . . .

He hesitated a little more; then he stood up. He took one step forward. I couldn't move.

There was nothing more than a flash of yellow close to his ankle. He stood motionless for a moment. He did not cry out. He fell as gently as a tree falls. There was not even the slightest sound, because of the sand.

CHAPTER TWENTY-SEVEN

And now, six years have already gone by . . . I have never before told this story. The companions who met me when I returned were glad to see me alive. I was sad but told them I was tired . . . '

Now I have overcome part of my sorrow. In other words, I have recovered but not entirely. I do know that he has gone back to his planet because I did not find his body at daybreak. It wasn't such a heavy body, after all . . . And I love to listen to the stars at night. It is like listening to five hundred million little bells . . .

But one thing worries me. When I drew the muzzle for the little prince, I forgot to add the leather strap to it. He will never be able to fasten it to his sheep. So I keep wondering what has happened on his planet. Perhaps the sheep has eaten the flower . . .

From time to time, I say to myself: 'Surely not! The little prince covers his flower every night with her glass dome and watches his sheep carefully . . .' Then I am happy. And all the stars laugh softly.

But then I think: 'Everyone can be absent-minded at times and it only takes once. He forgot the glass dome one evening or the sheep slipped out noiselessly during the night . . . ' And the little bells all change themselves into tears . . .

This is indeed a great mystery. For those of you who, like me, love the little prince, nothing in the universe can be the same while somewhere, nobody knows where, a sheep which we have never seen may or may not have eaten a flower . . .

Look at the sky. Ask yourselves: Has the sheep eaten the flower, yes or no? And you will see how everything changes . . .

And no grown-ups will ever understand why it is so important!

This is to me the most beautiful and saddest landscape in the world. It is the same landscape as in the last picture but I have drawn it once again to impress it upon your memory. It is here that the little prince appeared on Earth and then disappeared.

Look very carefully at the landscape so as to be sure to recognise it if ever one day you travel to Africa, through the desert. And if you should happen to come upon this spot, please do not hurry on. Wait a little, exactly under the star. Then, if a child comes towards you, if he laughs, if he has golden locks and if he refuses to answer questions, you will surely guess who he is. So be kind! Do not leave me grieving. Write to me quickly to tell me that he has come back . . .